Deep Space Discovery

THE SEARCH FOR NEW PLANETS

GAIL TERP

BLACK
RABBIT
BOOKS

Bolt is published by Black Rabbit Books
P.O. Box 3263, Mankato, Minnesota, 56002.
www.blackrabbitbooks.com
Copyright © 2019 Black Rabbit Books

Marysa Storm, editor; Grant Gould, designer;
Omay Ayres, photo researcher

Library of Congress Cataloging-in-Publication Data
Names: Terp, Gail, 1951- author.
Title: The search for new planets / by Gail Terp.
Description: Mankato, Minnesota : Black Rabbit Books, [2019] | Series:
Bolt. Deep space discovery | Audience: Age 9-12. | Audience: Grade 4 to
6. | Includes bibliographical references and index.
Identifiers: LCCN 2017022880 (print) | LCCN 2017037526 (ebook) |
ISBN 9781680725391 (ebook) | ISBN 9781680724233 (library binding) |
9781680727173 (paperback)
Subjects: LCSH: Extrasolar planets–Juvenile literature. | Planets–Juvenile
literature.
Classification: LCC QB820 (ebook) | LCC QB820 .T47 2019 (print) |
DDC 523.2/4-dc23
LC record available at https://lccn.loc.gov/2017022880

Printed in China. 3/18

Image Credits

Alamy: Dimitar Todorov, 22; JPL-
CALTECH/NASA/SPL, 10; Mark Garlick, 17
(bttm); National Geographic Creative, 28 (bttm);
Panther Media GmbH, Cover (astronaut); Science
Photo Library, 19; jwst.nasa.gov: JWST/NASA, 16–17, 27
(James Webb Telescopes); nasa.gov: NASA, 13, 14, 16 (bttm);
NASA/JPL-Caltech, 12; NASA Ames/SETI Institute/JPL-Caltech,
4–5, 17 (top); pitzer.caltech.edu, JPL/NASA, 16 (top); Shutter-
stock: Azuzl, 27 (earth); clearviewstock, 25; cigdem, 6–7; Dotted
Yeti, 9; Filipe Frazao, 20 (earth); foxaon1987, 3, 32; Harvepino,
20–21 (bkgd); Johan Swanepoel, 20 (core); Marc Ward, 21;
Natykach Nataliia, 31; Neo Edmund, 1; Vadim Sadovski, Cover
(bkgd), 28 (full pg); Yuriy Mazur, 26–27 (starry bkgd); wfirst.
gsfc.nasa.gov: NASA, 26–27 (Survey telescopes)
Every effort has been made to contact copyright
holders for material reproduced in this book. Any
omissions will be rectified in subsequent
printings if notice is given to the
publisher.

CONTENTS

CHAPTER 1

The Solar System and

In 2014, **astronomers** made an amazing discovery. They found Kepler-186f, a new planet. The planet is Earth-sized. It's also in its star's habitable zone. Being in this zone means it could have liquid water. The planet might be rocky too. And if a rocky planet has water, it might have life!

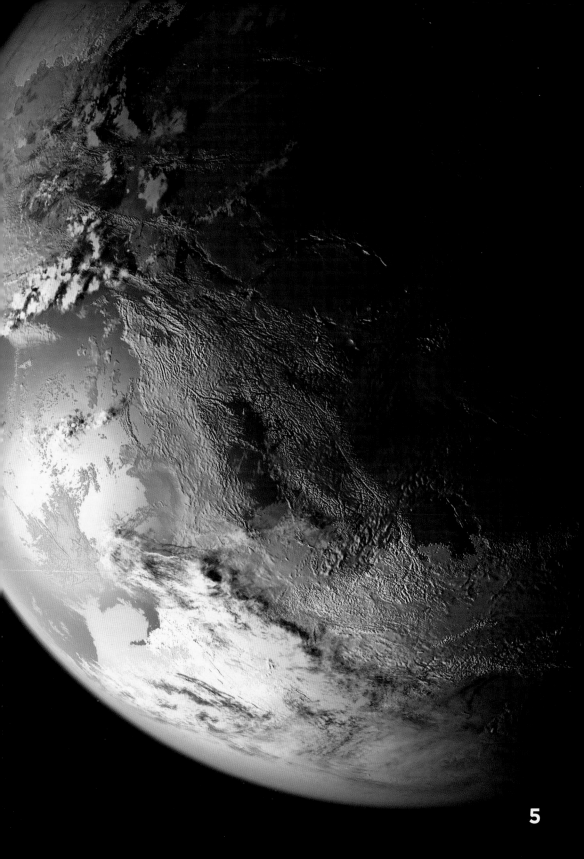

5

The Three Rules for Planets

Bodies in space must follow three rules to be called planets.

RULE ONE
It must orbit a star.

RULE TWO
It must be mostly round.

RULE THREE
Its path must be clear of smaller objects.

Planets

Planets are large bodies that orbit stars. Stars' **gravity** holds planets in their paths.

Earth and seven other planets circle the sun. They make up Earth's solar system.

Beyond Earth's Solar System

Earth's solar system isn't the only solar system in space. Other planets, such as Kepler-186f, orbit stars too. Scientists call planets outside Earth's solar system exoplanets. Today, scientists study exoplanets. They work to discover new ones.

artist's idea of what an
exoplanet might look like

CHAPTER 2

Discovering

In 1992, scientists discovered the first two exoplanets. They orbited a pulsar. A pulsar is a dead star. In 1995, astronomers found the first exoplanet orbiting a sunlike star. Since then, scientists have confirmed more than 3,400 exoplanets.

Telescopes

Scientists use telescopes to find new planets. Not all telescopes are used on the ground, though. Some are sent into space. Telescopes in space can see much farther. In 1990, NASA sent the Hubble Space Telescope into space. Other telescopes soon followed. They've helped discover hundreds of exoplanets.

Space Telescopes Used to Study Exoplanets

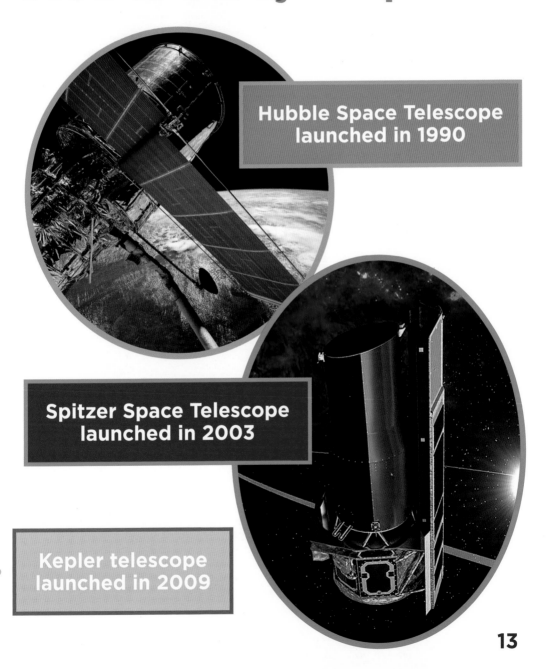

Hubble Space Telescope launched in 1990

Spitzer Space Telescope launched in 2003

Kepler telescope launched in 2009

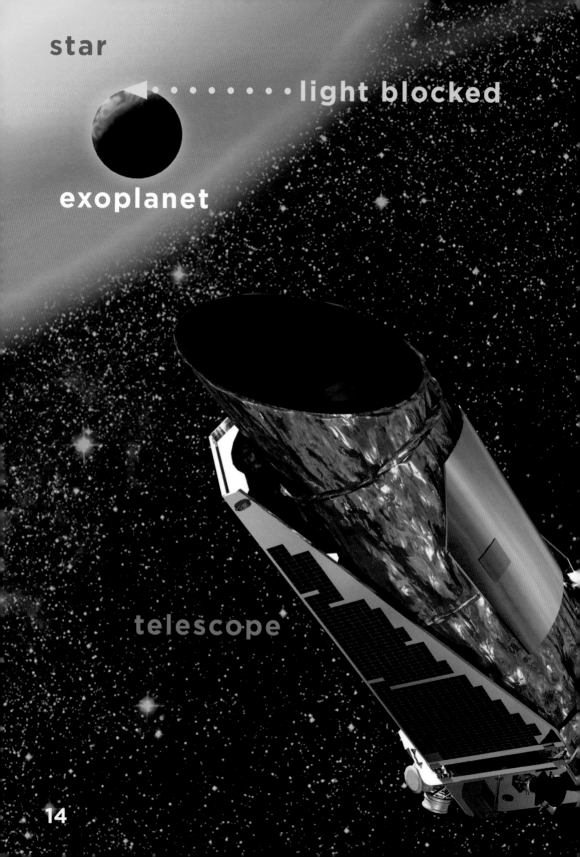

star

exoplanet

light blocked

telescope

Transits

Exoplanets are very far away and hard to find. They are darker and smaller than stars. But there are ways to find them. One way is the transit method. An exoplanet may pass between its star and a telescope. When it does, the exoplanet blocks some of the star's light. Telescopes can spot this change in light. The amount of light that's blocked tells scientists the size of the exoplanet.

THE SEARCH FOR EXOPLANETS

2007
Astronomers use the Spitzer to map an exoplanet.

1992
Scientists announce the discovery of the first two exoplanets.

1990

1995
Astronomers discover the first exoplanet around a sunlike star.

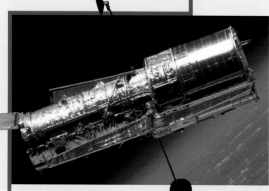

2001
Scientists use the Hubble to study an exoplanet's **atmosphere**.

2014

Astronomers discover the first Earth-sized exoplanet that might support life.

2020

2017

NASA discovers a new solar system. It's about 40 light-years from Earth.

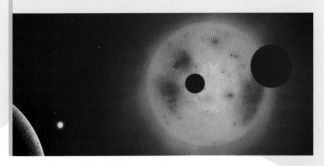

2019

The James Webb Space Telescope enters space.
(Launch plan as of January 2018.)

Life on Other Planets?

The first exoplanets scientists discovered couldn't support life. Some are too hot. Others are made of gas. Then scientists discovered Kepler-186f. Scientists don't know if it supports life. But it's the first exoplanet discovered that could. Scientists have since found other planets that might support life.

Kepler-186f orbits a red dwarf. Light from the star is orange-red.

WHAT DOES A PLANET NEED TO SUPPORT LIFE?

In order to have life, scientists believe a planet must have these traits.

perfect distance from a star

heat-melted core that maintains magnetic field

atmosphere

liquid water ·····▶

surface made
of rock ·······▶

protective
magnetic
field ·········▶

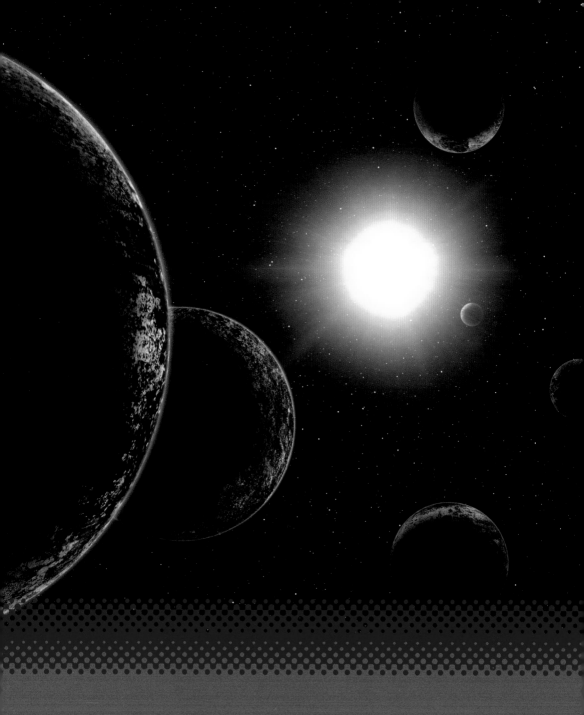

A light-year measures distance. It's how far light travels in one year. One light-year is about 5.9 trillion miles (9.5 trillion kilometers).

A New Planet System

In 2017, astronomers found a new solar system. It has seven planets. They circle the star TRAPPIST-1. It is about 40 light-years from Earth. Each of its planets is about the size of Earth. Three are at the right distance from the star to have liquid water. They are probably rocky too. Could they have life?

CHAPTER 3

The Future in

SPACE

Scientists will keep studying exoplanets. The James Webb telescope will be a useful tool. The Wide-Field Infrared Survey Telescope will be too. It should enter space in the 2020s. The powerful telescope will continue the search for new planets.

Wide-Field Infrared Survey Telescope

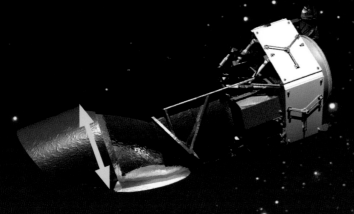

main mirror diameter
7.9 feet
(2 meters)

Mission Goals

James Webb Space Telescope
Study the history of the **universe** and the formation of other solar systems.

Wide-Field Infrared Survey Telescope
Discover exoplanets and research dark energy.

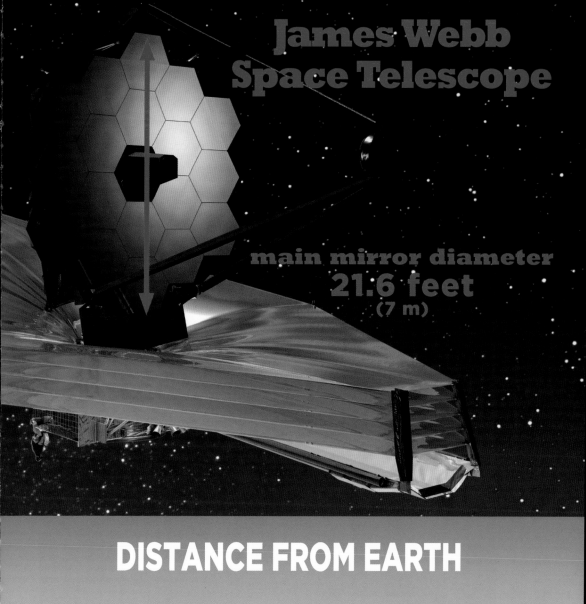

James Webb Space Telescope

main mirror diameter
21.6 feet
(7 m)

DISTANCE FROM EARTH

James Webb Space Telescope
about 1 million miles
(1,609,344 km)

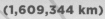

Wide-Field Infrared Survey Telescope
about 1 million miles
(1,609,344 km)

Reaching for the Stars

Scientists hope to send spacecraft to exoplanets. The trips will take years. The new spacecraft must be fast and strong. Their **fuel** must last a long time too.

Each mission will bring new knowledge. Maybe one will discover signs of life!

A spacecraft took about 36 years just to leave Earth's solar system.

astronomer (uh-STRON-uh-mer)—
an expert in the science of heavenly
bodies and of their sizes, motions,
and composition

atmosphere (AT-muh-sfeer)—the gases
that surround a planet

core (KOHR)—the central part of a planet
or other body

fuel (FEYUL)—a material, such as coal,
oil, or gas, that is burned to produce heat
or power

gravity (GRAV-i-tee)—the natural force
that pulls physical things toward each other

magnetic field (mag-NE-tik FEELD)—an
area where an object's magnetic properties
affect neighboring objects

orbit (AWR-bit)—the path taken by one
body circling around another body

trait (TREYT)—a characteristic or quality

universe (YOO-nuh-vurs)—all of space
and everything in it

BOOKS

Fretland VanVoorst, Jenny. *Spacecraft.* Space Explorers. Minneapolis: Pogo, 2016.

Lakin, Patricia. *The Stellar Story of Space Travel.* History of Fun Stuff. New York: Simon Spotlight, 2016.

Stargazing to Space Travel: A Timeline of Space Exploration. A Timeline Of ... Chicago: World Book, Inc., a Scott Fetzer Company, 2016.

WEBSITES

All about Exoplanets
spaceplace.nasa.gov/all-about-exoplanets/en/

Are We Alone?
www.esa.int/esaKIDSen/Arewealone.html

History of Space Travel
kids.nationalgeographic.com/explore/space/history-of-space-travel/#space-first-space-suit.jpg

INDEX